THIS BOOK BELONGS TO

_____

PEANUTS

A Charlie Brown
CHRISTMAS

YEARS
— A CHARLIE BROWN —
CHRISTMAS

By Charles M. Schulz

Based on the animated special, the text was adapted by Tina Gallo

Illustrated by Scott Jeralds

Simon Spotlight

New York   London   Toronto   Sydney   New Delhi

SIMON SPOTLIGHT

An imprint of Simon & Schuster Children's Publishing Division

1230 Avenue of the Americas, New York, New York 10020

First Simon Spotlight edition September 2015

SIMON SPOTLIGHT and colophon are registered trademarks of Simon & Schuster, Inc. For information about special discounts for bulk purchases, please contact Simon & Schuster Special Sales at 1-866-506-1949 or business@simonandschuster.com. Manufactured in China 0715 SCP

10 9 8 7 6 5 4 3 2 1   ISBN 978-1-4814-4432-3   ISBN 978-1-4814-4433-0 (eBook)

It's the most magical time of the year. Christmas is coming! The air is crisp and cold, children are ice-skating, and the sound of Christmas carols fills the air. Everyone is in the holiday spirit.

Well, almost everyone.

"I think there must be something wrong with me," Charlie Brown says. "Christmas is coming, but I'm not happy. I like getting presents, sending cards, decorating trees, and all that, but I always end up feeling sad."

"Charlie Brown, you're the only person I know who can take a wonderful season like Christmas and turn it into a problem," Linus says. "Maybe Lucy's right. Of all the Charlie Browns in the world, you're the Charlie Browniest."

Charlie Brown decides to talk to Lucy. She gives really good advice, and it only costs five cents.

"I just don't understand Christmas," Charlie Brown tells her. "Instead of feeling happy, I feel sort of let down."

"You need to get involved in a real Christmas project," Lucy advises. "How would you like to be the director of our Christmas play?"

"Me? A director?" Charlie Brown is surprised at the suggestion. He knows nothing about directing, but it sounds exciting! He agrees to meet Lucy at the school auditorium.

On his way to the auditorium, Charlie Brown spots his dog, Snoopy, carrying a box of Christmas ornaments and lights. He watches as Snoopy carefully decorates his doghouse. Snoopy has entered a contest to win money for the best neighborhood Christmas lights and display.

"My own dog has gone commercial!" Charlie Brown groans. "I can't stand it!"

Next, Charlie Brown is stopped by his sister, Sally. "Will you help me write a letter to Santa Claus, big brother?" Sally asks.

Charlie Brown begins to write down everything Sally says.

"Dear Santa Claus," Sally starts. "How have you been? I have been extra good this year, so I have a long list of presents. But you can make it easy on yourself. Just send money! How about tens and twenties?"

Charlie Brown sighs. "Good grief!"

When Charlie Brown finally arrives at the auditorium, the cast is waiting for him. "Okay, let's have quiet!" he announces. "Places, everybody. Action."

But no one listens to him. Schroeder starts playing his piano and everyone starts dancing. Nobody cares that Charlie Brown is directing. Nobody cares about the play. They just want to dance!

Charlie Brown feels even worse than he did before. “This Christmas play is all wrong,” he moans.

Lucy tries to make him feel better. “Everybody knows Christmas is just a time of year for people to buy stuff,” she says.

But Charlie Brown disagrees. “This is one play that is going to be different. We need something to set the proper mood. We need a Christmas tree!”

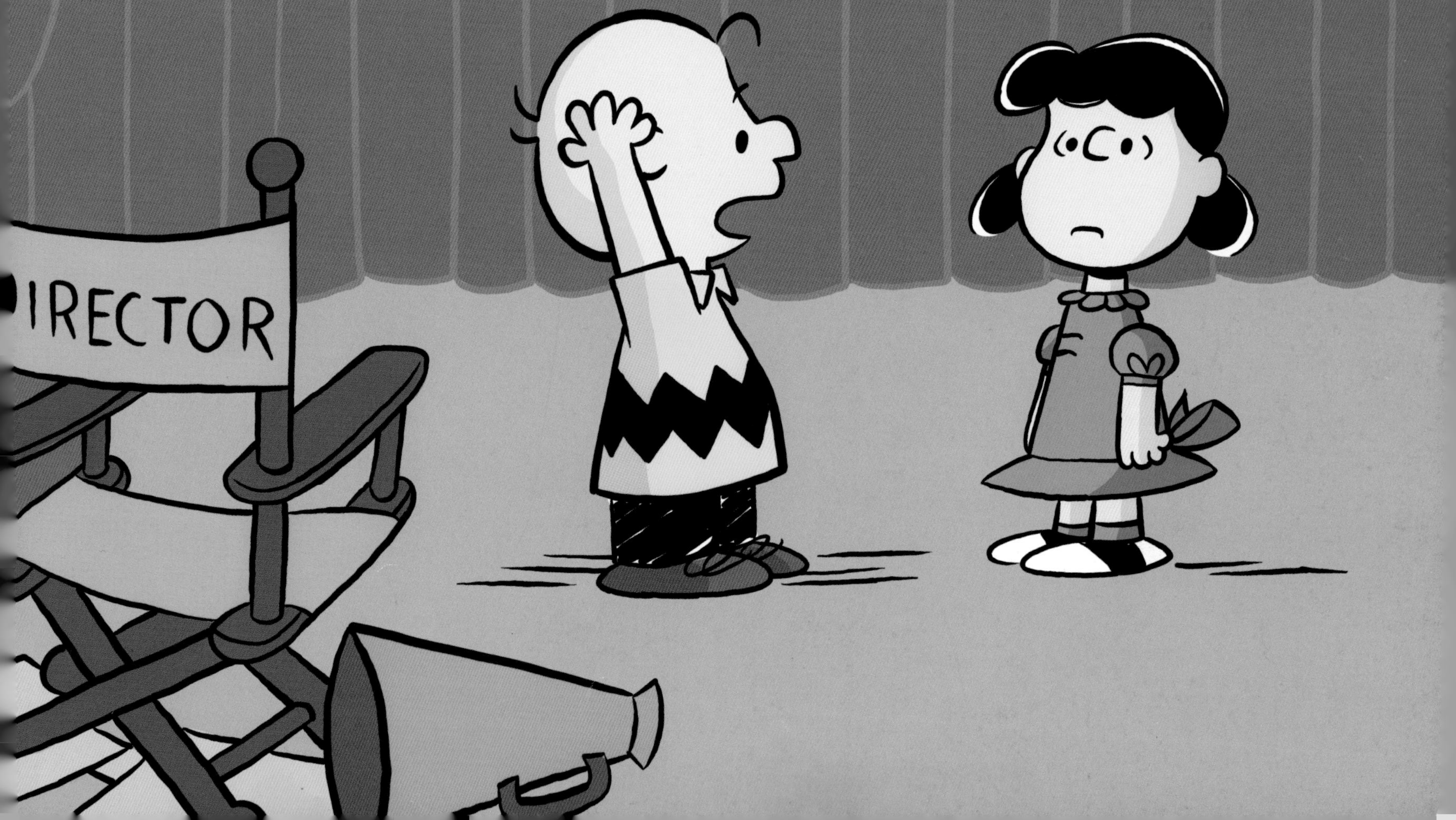
IRECTOR

"That's it!" Lucy exclaims. "We need a Christmas tree! A great, big, shiny aluminum tree! You go get the tree, Charlie Brown."

"I'll take Linus with me," Charlie Brown says. "The rest of you can practice your lines."

Lucy is excited about the Christmas tree. "Get the biggest aluminum tree you can find," she orders. "Maybe painted pink!"

When Charlie Brown and Linus arrive at the Christmas tree lot, they are surrounded by fake trees. Some are plastic. Some are aluminum. Some are painted different colors. Some even have polka dots.

Linus knocks on one of the aluminum trees. "Do they still make wooden Christmas trees?" he wonders out loud. Meanwhile, Charlie Brown is starting to feel sad again. None of these trees feel right to him.

Then Charlie Brown sees it. A teeny-tiny green tree. He smiles. "This little tree seems to need a home," he says.

Linus hesitates. "I don't know, Charlie Brown. This doesn't seem to fit the modern spirit."

But Charlie Brown suddenly feels better than he has in days. "We'll decorate it, and it will be just right for our play. Besides, I think it needs me." He picks up the tree.

Needles tinkle as they fall off the scrawny tree, making it even scrawnier.

Charlie Brown is still smiling when he returns to the auditorium. He gently places the tree down on Schroeder's piano. "We're back!" he announces. Everyone rushes over to see the tree. They are shocked and disappointed at Charlie Brown's choice.

"You were supposed to get a good tree!" Lucy declares. "Can't you even tell a good tree from a poor tree?"

Everyone agrees.

What happens next is worst of all. Everybody starts to laugh at Charlie Brown and the little tree—even Snoopy!

Charlie Brown feels sadder than ever. He turns to Linus. "I guess you were right," he says. "I shouldn't have picked this little tree. I really don't know what Christmas is all about." He pauses and looks around. "Isn't there *anyone* who knows what Christmas is all about?" he cries.

To his surprise, it is Linus who answers. "Sure, Charlie Brown. I can tell you what Christmas is all about." He walks to the center of the stage and says, "Lights, please."

Somebody dims the lights in the auditorium and puts a single spotlight on Linus. In a clear voice, Linus begins to speak.

"And there were shepherds abiding in the field, keeping watch over their flock by night. And the Angel of the Lord came upon them and said, 'Fear not: for behold, I bring you tidings of great joy. For unto you is born this day a Savior, which is Christ the Lord.' And there was with the angel a multitude of the heavenly host praising God and saying, 'Glory to God; peace on Earth, good will to men.'"

Everyone is quiet as Linus finishes. "That's what Christmas is all about, Charlie Brown," he says.

Charlie Brown picks up his little tree and steps outside. He looks up at the dark sky full of twinkling stars. He finally feels happy deep down inside, the way Christmas is supposed to make you feel.

"Linus is right," he says to himself. "I'm not going to let everyone else's greed spoil my Christmas. I'll take this little tree home and decorate it, and show everyone it really will work in our play."

Charlie Brown passes Snoopy's fully decorated doghouse. Snoopy won first prize! He takes a shiny red ornament off the doghouse and hangs it on the little tree.

But the ornament is too heavy, and the little tree topples over.

Charlie Brown is horrified. "I've killed it!" he cries. "Everything I touch gets ruined." He walks away sadly, with his head down, leaving the little tree alone.

After Charlie Brown leaves, the others find the tree.

"I never thought it was such a bad little tree," Linus says. He wraps his blanket around the tree's base. "It's not bad at all, really. All it needs is a little love."

Without saying a word, the other kids begin taking the decorations off of Snoopy's doghouse and putting them on the tree.

It doesn't take long for them to transform the little tree into something magical!

When Charlie Brown returns a few minutes later, he can scarcely believe his eyes.

First he looks at Snoopy's bare doghouse, then at the beautiful tree. "What's going on here?" he asks. Then he looks at his friends. Their faces are all shining with joy.

"Merry Christmas, Charlie Brown!" they shout. And before Charlie Brown can say another word, they start to sing Christmas carols.

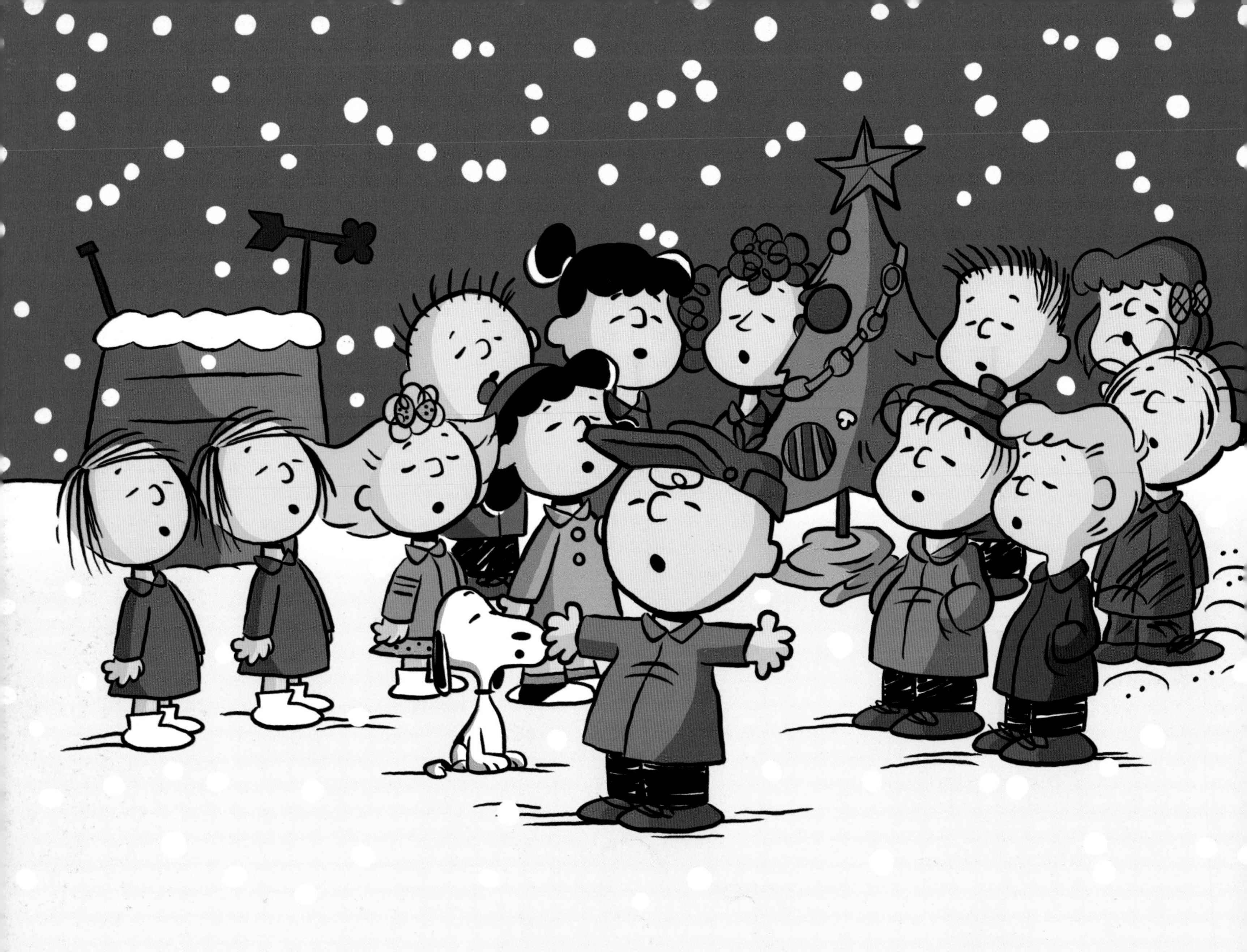

Charlie Brown smiles and starts singing with his friends. He knows it is going to be the best Christmas ever!

HAPPY HOLIDAYS FROM SNOOPY